EVERYBODY SLEEPS (BUT NOT Fred)

CLARION BOOKS
HOUGHTON MIFFLIN HARCOURT
Boston   New York

Clarion Books
215 Park Avenue South
New York, New York 10003

Copyright © 2015 by Josh Schneider

Clarion Books is an imprint of Houghton Mifflin Harcourt Publishing Company.

www.hmhco.com

The text was set in ScalaSans.
The illustrations in this book were done in watercolor and pen and ink.

Library of Congress Cataloging-in-Publication Data
Schneider, Josh, 1980– author, illustrator.
Everybody sleeps (but not Fred) / Josh Schneider.
pages cm
Summary: Although animals everywhere are sleeping,
a youngster with an active imagination and a hefty to-do list
resists bedtime with adventurous flair.
ISBN 978-0-544-33924-8 (hardcover)
[1. Stories in rhyme. 2. Bedtime—Fiction.
3. Animals—Sleep behavior—Fiction.] I. Title.
PZ8.3.S297185Ev 2015
[E]—dc23
2014021777

Manufactured in China
SCP 10 9 8 7 6 5 4 3 2 1
4500512278

To Dana, who rarely mentions my snoring.

Every kind of bird and beast,
in the West and in the East,
way up high and way down deep,
everybody has to sleep.

But not Fred. Fred has a to-do list you wouldn't believe.

98. WRESTLE A BEAR
99. EAT 300 COOKIES
100. GO TO MOON

In the jungle, toucans snooze.
Also sloths and cockatoos.
Ignoring snoring striped hyenas,
monkeys dream they're ballerinas.

But not Fred.

Fred has important jumping to do.

On the farm, the chickens doze.
The pigs nod off in stinky rows.
Sheep lie in a woolly heap,
count themselves, and fall asleep.

SHEEP COUNT
M: ~~HHT~~ III
Tu: ~~HHT~~ III
W: ~~HHT~~ III
Th: ~~HHT~~ II Susan?
F: ~~HHT~~ III
Sat: ~~HHT~~ II
Sun: ~~HHT~~ III

10

But not Fred.

Fred is breaking the world shouting record.

'Neath the ocean, whales relax,
leaking bubbles fore and aft.
Rocked by currents in the deep,
ocean creatures go to sleep.

But not Fred.

Fred is testing his horn collection.

In their bunk beds underground,
tired ants have settled down.
Now too late to grab a snack,
anteaters all hit the sack.

But not Fred.

Fred is practicing his karate chops.

Scary things that lurk and slink
stop all that for forty winks,
like other creatures not here listed—
monsters, too (if they existed).

But not Fred.

Fred is hunting the legendary Sasquatch.

Having read a book or three,
parents turn to poetry,
reading from a book so boring,
children soon are prone and snoring.

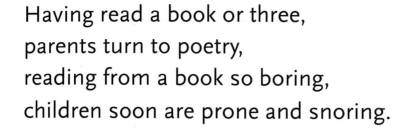

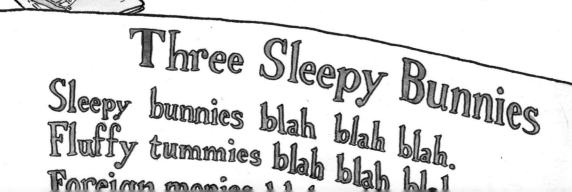

Three Sleepy Bunnies

Sleepy bunnies blah blah blah.
Fluffy tummies blah blah blah.
Foreign movies bl.

But not Fred.

Tumpty tumpty bunny benders.
tumpty money lenders.

Fred?

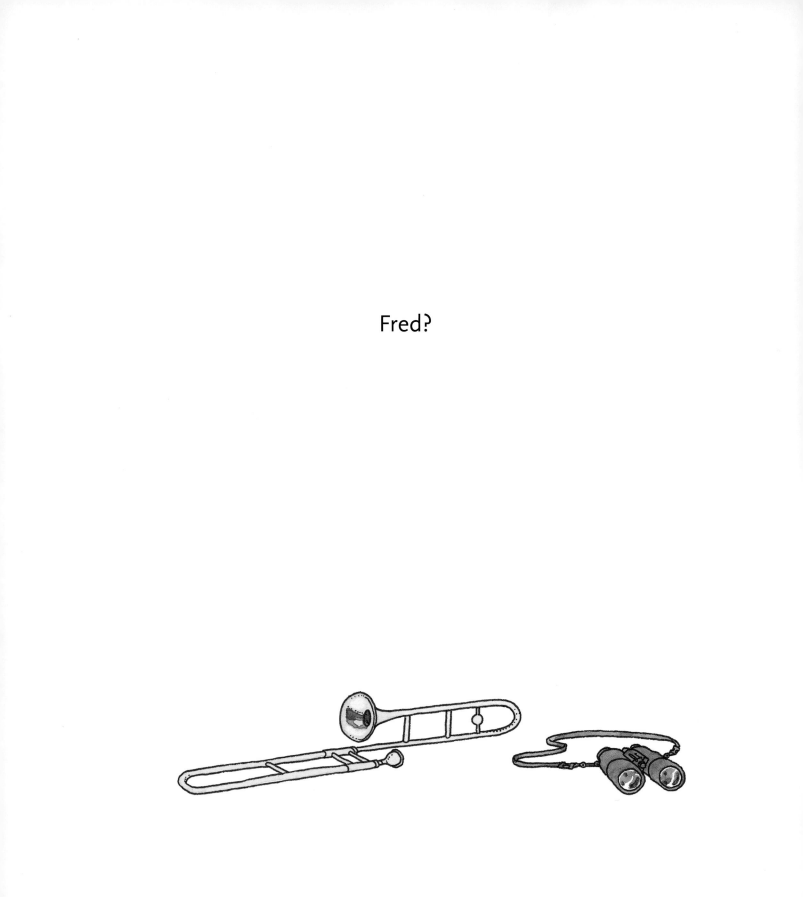

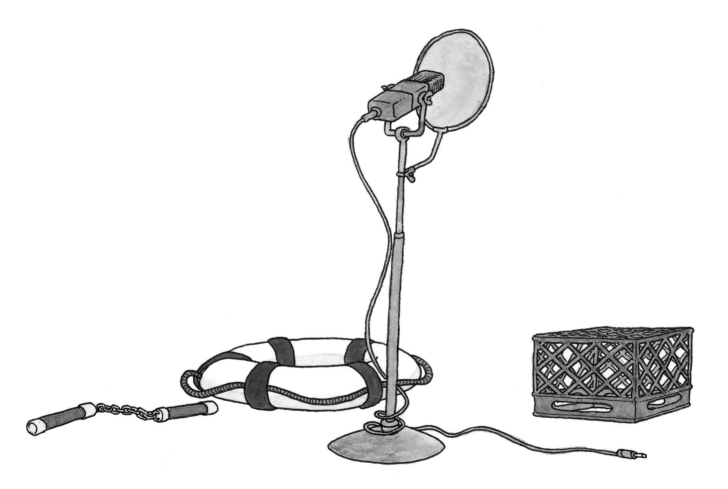

Tomorrow Fred will run about
and chop and jump and hunt and shout.
But please, for now don't make a peep.
Just close the book and let Fred sleep.

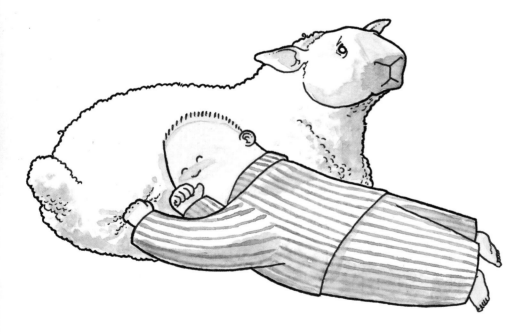

WARNING

CLOSE BOOK SOFTLY
OR FRED WILL WAKE UP
AND START ALL
OVER AGAIN.

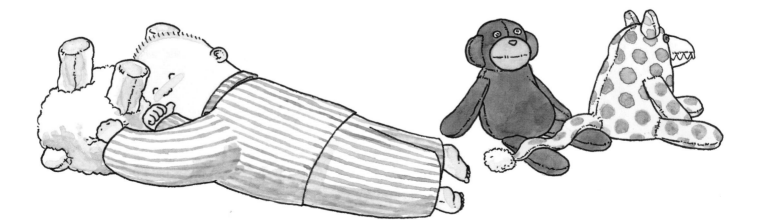